AND THE PIRATE PUZZLE

Bath · New York · Singapore · Hong Kong · Cologne · Delhi · Melbourne

Written by Zed Storm
Creative concept and words by E. Hawken
Check out the website at www.will-solvit.com

First edition published by Parragon in 2010

Parragon
Queen Street House
4 Queen Street
Bath BA1 1HE, UK

ISBN 978-1-4454-0459-2

Printed in China

Please retain this information for future reference.

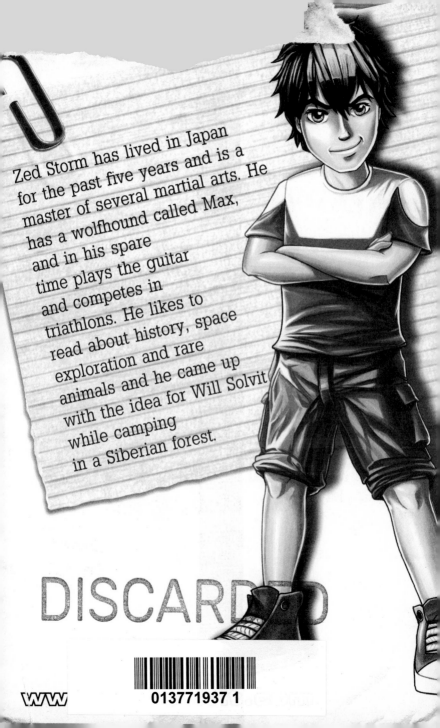

Zed Storm has lived in Japan for the past five years and is a master of several martial arts. He has a wolfhound called Max, and in his spare time plays the guitar and competes in triathlons. He likes to read about history, space exploration and rare animals and he came up with the idea for Will Solvit while camping in a Siberian forest.

DISCARDED

ATTENTION: ALL READERS!

Wherever you see something that looks like this, reach for your decoder! Holding it by the right side, place the centre of your decoder over the lines. Rotate it very slowly, look closely and a picture will appear.

Mystery solved!

CONTENTS

CHAPTER ONE
BEEF AND CHOCOLATE STEW - YUM!

"Dinner is served," Grandpa beamed proudly, placing a bowl of beef and chocolate stew in front of me.

"Er, thanks, Grandpa," I smiled. I've been living with Grandpa Monty since my parents went missing, and I'm used to his crazy cooking. Beef and chocolate stew is actually quite a normal dinner dish at Grandpa's house – he once cooked me grasshoppers with kidney custard!

"Grandpa," I said, stuffing a spoonful of meaty-choc stew into my hungry mouth, "I've just had an awesome clue about how I can find Mum."

"Don't speak with your mouth full, Oliver."

Grandpa always calls me by the wrong name, and he always ignores me when I try to talk to him about Adventures.

I'm a time-travelling Adventurer, you see. I get special letters with clues that tell me what mysteries need to be solved and how I need to solve them. So far my Adventures have taken me to some amazing places – like back to ancient Egypt, a future ruled by droid penguins, the time of cannibal cavemen and even back to old-school Japan where I battled ninjas!

But my Adventures have never taken me to what I want most in the entire history of time and space – my parents.

Grandpa bent down to feed his dog Plato some left-over beef from the stew. Plato nibbled it cautiously before swallowing it down in one gulp – he's as suspicious of Grandpa's food as I am.

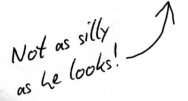

Not as silly as he looks!

"Zoe's mother called a minute ago," said Grandpa, sitting down at the table next to me and opening up a newspaper. "She needs to go back into work this evening so Zoe's coming here to stay the night. Stanley is upstairs making up a guest bedroom in the West Wing for her right now."

OK, a few things I need to explain:

1. Zoe is my best friend (she's a girl, but she's cool).
2. Zoe lives with her mum cuz her dad lives in Singapore.
3. Zoe knows that I'm an Adventurer.
4. Stanley is Grandpa's butler.
5. Solvit Hall is HUGE – the West Wing is just one area of many empty rooms.

I sighed into my stew as Grandpa told me Zoe was coming over. Zoe's my best friend but I had just said goodbye to her a few hours before, when she'd been kidnapped by ancient knights and taken back in time. I had rescued her and was, until now, looking forward to spending some time on my own, looking over my last clue.

"Does she have to come over?" I whinged.

At that moment the front doorbell rang.

Zoe had arrived.

"I'll get it!" Stanley called, walking towards the door.

I let out a huge belch as Zoe walked in.

"Will, that's disgusting!" Zoe complained, screwing up her nose at me.

"I'd been saving that for you!" I said jokingly.

"Dinner?" Grandpa asked Zoe.

Girls just DON'T get it!

Belly belching rocks!

"No thanks, Monty," Zoe said politely. "I've already eaten."

Zoe's mega-smart – she knows better than to risk eating one of Grandpa's meals.

"I've come to help you find your mum," Zoe said quietly, so Grandpa couldn't hear. "I've brought food – normal food – and a load of stuff I printed off the internet about the Seismic Square in 1804."

"Nice one, Zoe," I said, gratefully. I felt bad for not wanting her to come over earlier. She really is a brilliant friend.

"Grandpa," I said loudly. "We're going to travel back in time to find my mum."

"Know where you're going, do you?" Grandpa asked, without looking up from his newspaper.

"Sure!" I smiled.

Zoe and I ran from the kitchen and headed

upstairs to pack more things for our Adventure.

"Check this out," I said, handing her my diary, where I'd been keeping the clues that will lead me to Mum and Dad.

Zoe read the last few diary entries quickly.

THE DIARY AND
CLUE RECORD OF
WILL SOLVIT, ADVENTURER

CLUES
- Mum is stuck in the Seismic Square in the year 1804.
- Mum is known as the Seismic Siren.
- I will find Mum after a long journey at sea.

PLAN OF ACTION
- Time travel back to 1804.
- Find a boat that will take me to the Seismic Square.

- Find Mum in the Seismic Square.
- Bring Mum back to land.
- Time travel back to the present day.
- Find Dad.

While Zoe caught up on what I knew about Mum's whereabouts, I packed for the journey ahead. I stuffed my backpack with the best Adventuring tools I could find. This is what I took:

- Camouflage paint
- Four omnilumes (they're these really cool glow sticks that can turn night to day)
- Night vision goggles
- Walkie-talkie ear plugs
- Invisibility paint
- Compass that always points home

- Bottle of truth serum
- Electric stun gun
- Pen that can write in any language
- Morph's discs

Morph is my dad's greatest-ever invention that can turn into anything, including a time machine. I activated it and stood back as it spun into life, its motors whirring and buzzing with excitement. Morph transformed into a time machine right there in my bedroom.

"Ready?" I smiled at Zoe.

"As I'll ever be!" she grinned back.

We stepped into Morph and closed the door.

"Take me to 1804!" I shouted, hoping it would do as it was told, for once. (Morph usually took me to where I needed to be and not where I wanted to be.)

Zoom!

The time machine began to
shake violently. I screwed my eyes tight shut and
tried to ignore the sick feeling in my stomach.

Time travelling is like a rollercoaster x 10!

The sound of gushing air and years of history
filled my ears as Morph travelled back in time.

Suddenly, we ground to a halt and landed with
a thud.

I opened my eyes.

"You OK?" I asked Zoe.

"Time travelling doesn't get any easier, does
it?" she replied, looking slightly green.

I opened the time machine's door and held
my breath.

The first thing I saw was a man.

The man was dressed in an old-fashioned
military uniform. He was wearing white trousers,
shiny leather boots, a red coat with gold buttons

and a large, triangular hat.

He took his hat off and saluted me, revealing short, light-brown hair.

"Captain Luke Solvit at your service," he said. "This arrived for you by carrier pigeon this morning." He reached into his hat and pulled out a white envelope with my name on it.

"Hi," I said, cautiously taking the letter from him. "I'm Will – I'm a Solvit too. We must be related. How did you know about me?"

"Pleased to make your acquaintance, Will," Luke smiled broadly. "The carrier pigeon brought a letter for me too. The letter told me you'd arrive here at this time and it told me that I'm to assist you with your Adventure. I'm an airship fleet commander. What do you do?"

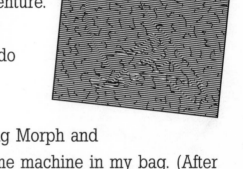

"Time travel," I replied, deactivating Morph and putting the mini time machine in my bag. (After use, Morph shrinks into a small version of the last thing it's used for.) "This is Zoe," I said.

"Hi," Zoe grinned, "I didn't know airships existed in 1804."

"Nor do most people," Luke replied. "And I'd appreciate it if you kept the secret to yourselves."

"It's OK," Zoe assured him. "I'm good at

keeping Adventure secrets." Then she turned to me and said, "Aren't you going to open your letter, Will?"

I ripped open the envelope and read the letter inside. This is what it said:

WHAT'S HIGHER THAN AN AIRSHIP FLEET COMMANDER?
AN AIRSHIP FLEET COMMANDER'S HAT!

CAPTAIN LUKE SOLVIT WILL FLY YOU TO THE PORT OF LOST SOULS.
THIS ADVENTURE WILL LEAD YOU TO SOMETHING YOU HAVE GREATLY MISSED.
YOU'VE EARNED THE RIGHT TO BE REUNITED WITH YOUR MOTHER.

I didn't need to be a mind reader to see Captain Luke's terror as I read out my letter.

"W...w...why would anyone want to travel to the Port of Lost Souls?" he stuttered.

"I'm guessing that's where we need to go to set sail for the Seismic Square," I answered, looking around. We were standing in a large field next to a huge old-fashioned airship.

The airship had a large balloon and propeller at the top and a small

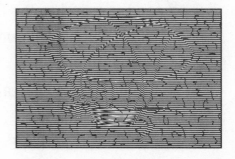

metal basket at the bottom – it didn't look very safe. Along the side of the metal basket were the words 'The Godfather'.

"Is The Godfather one of the airships in your fleet?" Zoe asked, walking towards the ship to get a better look.

"My best ship," Luke answered distractedly before turning to me. "Excuse me, too many years of high-altitude sailing has affected my ears," he chuckled slightly. "For a brief moment there, Will, I thought I heard you say that you wished to sail to the Seismic Square."

"I do need to travel to the Seismic Square," I replied. A look of horror swept across Luke's face.

"Is this thing safe?" Zoe called, clambering into the basket of Luke's ship.

"Those who sail into the Seismic Square never

return," Luke said gravely, ignoring Zoe.

"Look," I said. "I think we kinda got off on the wrong foot here. You gotta trust me on this one – I know what I'm doing, I'll be fine."

"True Adventurer spirit," Luke smiled, putting his hat back on. "I will take you wherever you need to go – and the Port of Lost Souls is indeed the last land before ships set sail towards the Seismic Square." Luke looked me up and down, studying my jeans, T-shirt and backpack. "What are airships and ships like in the future?" he asked excitedly.

"I'll tell you all about the future if you tell me everything you know about the Seismic Square," I said. I pointed to The Godfather. "But we need to get a move on. I don't want to waste any more time standing here chatting when I should be rescuing my mum."

True Adventurer spirit!

"Your mother is missing?" questioned Luke, walking towards the airship.

I quickly told him all about Mum, about how she and Dad had gone missing in a prehistoric jungle filled with dinosaurs, and how they'd somehow become separated in time and space and that it was up to me to find them both.

We climbed into the metal basket at the bottom of The Godfather. Zoe and I stood back as Captain Luke lit a fire that roared upwards towards the balloon above us. Soon the balloon filled with hot air and the airship's propellers started to whir into action.

Before I knew it, The Godfather had lifted off the ground and started to drift through the sky.

"It's a long way down," Zoe said nervously, peering over the basket edge to the ground far below.

Feeling a bit queasy! ︶

"I wouldn't lean too far over the edge if I were you!" Luke told her. "Airships have a habit of swinging from side to side. I wouldn't want you to fall to your death."

Zoe and I gulped. Luke's airship was cool but it didn't feel safe. Plus we had to shout to hear each other talk above the airship's engines . . .

Captain Luke continued shouting loudly.

"The only problem is how?" I muttered to myself.

"I'm afraid that's all I know about the Seismic Square and your mother," Luke said, talking more normally now as we got used to the noise. He turned to me and smiled. "Now it's your turn to tell me about the future!"

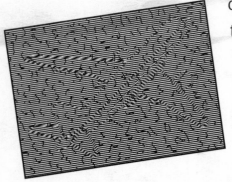

Between us, Zoe and I told Captain Luke all about cars and aeroplanes, televisions and computers, and anything else we could think of.

"I wish to visit

this future you talk of one day," he told us. Then he turned to the sky. "You see that shape in the distance?" he added, pointing to a blob of land on the horizon.

"Is it an island?" Zoe asked.

"It is the island where you will find the Port of Lost Souls. I cannot fly into the Seismic Square myself," he said. "I have other . . . Adventurer business to attend to."

"I understand," I nodded.

He nodded back at me, as if we were sharing some kind of unspoken Adventurer secret. "You will find someone in the Port of Lost Souls who will be willing to take you into the Seismic Square."

"If this place is as dangerous as you say it is," Zoe said, "who'd be mad enough to take us there?"

"There are those who care for money and wealth more than their safety," replied Luke.

"What kind of people can we pay to take us into certain doom?" I wondered.

"Pirates!" Luke replied. "Deadly, sea-hardy, gold-digging pirates. The Port of Lost Souls is full of them!"

Yo-ho-ho!

CHAPTER THREE
STINKY SAL'S TAVERN

The Godfather airship soared through the skies
towards the pirate island and the Port of Lost
Souls.

As we flew closer to land, the ground came into
focus and I could see sandy beaches, wooden huts
with flags flying high on the beaches and rickety
old piers leading from the island into the blue
sea. The island wasn't big – I could see the whole
thing from up in the air. Around the small island
were dozens of ships, each flapping a different
flag – I spotted at least ten ships with skulls and
crossbones on them!

"COMING IN
TO LAND!"

shouted Captain Luke at the top of his lungs.

Zoe and I clung onto the sides of the metal basket we were standing in as the airship's engines began to shriek loudly. Luke cut off the fire that was blasting into the balloon above us and we started to head towards the ground at super speed, but Luke somehow successfully steered the descending ship into an empty patch of sandy beach.

The impact of hitting the sand nearly threw me out of the airship. My whole body was vibrating – it felt just like time travelling!

The three of us climbed out of the airship's basket onto the golden sand. It was seriously hot – the sun was glaring down on my head.

Zoe and I watched as Captain Luke pulled a heavy metal anchor from The Godfather's basket and buried it in the sand.

"I'll take you to the port," he said, wiping the sand from his hands. "There's a tavern I know where you'll be able to find a pirate crew to take you into the Seismic Square."

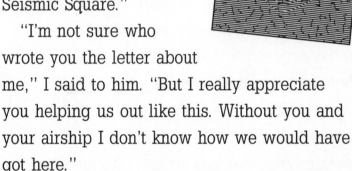

"I'm not sure who wrote you the letter about me," I said to him. "But I really appreciate you helping us out like this. Without you and your airship I don't know how we would have got here."

Luke smiled at me. "I've been getting letters ever since I became an Adventurer. Without those letters, there are many lives I could never have saved and many mysteries I would not have solved."

"Do you know who's sending you the letters?" Zoe asked quickly.

I held my breath, hoping Luke would give us an answer.

"No," he shook his head. I let out a frustrated sigh.

"I don't know who is sending them," he added, "but one letter told me that some day I would meet the person who wrote them."

"I wonder if you'll meet the person who's writing yours, Will," said Zoe, softly.

I shrugged.

Captain Luke began to trudge through the sand. We followed him up the beach, past some palm trees and out onto another beach.

This one was filled with people. Everyone was dressed in dirty, rag-like clothes and was either loading heavy-looking chests onto ships or

carrying them off onto the beach.

"What's going on?" Zoe asked.

"This port is where pirates come to off-load their booty," Luke said quietly, not wanting anyone else to hear. "You'd find a world of riches buried under the sands of this island – but you'd have to fight a pirate to the death if you ever wanted to take those riches away!"

We weaved our way between the crowds – no one paid us any attention. As Luke led us further inland, the golden sand turned into mud and we walked into what looked like a tiny shanty village surrounded by palm trees. He guided us down a dirt track towards a wooden shack with a badly put-together sign that read 'Stinky Sal's Tavern'.

"It be a while since I saw ye in these parts," grinned a woman walking towards Luke. She had about two teeth in her mouth – and those two teeth were as black as coal.

The woman spoke with a thick pirate accent, was wearing a torn dress and her hair looked like a bird had nested in it.

And she stank like a pile of dino dung!

"Give us a kiss . . ." She puckered up and plunged towards Luke. He ducked out of the way and she fell flat into the mud.

"That's Stinky Sal," he told us, stepping over her. "This is her tavern, only she doesn't really do much other than scare the customers away. She likes to drink rum – a lot of rum!"

Luke led us into Stinky Sal's Tavern.

It was dark in there and smelt like Stinky Sal's dirty armpit. Totally gross x 150!

Dim lanterns sat on wooden tables and lit the tavern. There were dozens of stinking pirates sitting on wooden stalls around the tables and drinking out of huge glasses.

Cats, dogs, monkeys, chickens and even goats were running over the filthy tavern floor – I had to watch every step I was taking in case I stood on one of them!

"What is this dump?" Zoe asked in disgust.

"This is where sailors and pirates come to tell their stories, trade their treasures and drink rum," Luke replied, stepping over a snoring man on the floor. He leaned over the bar to get the attention of one of the filthy barmaids.

"What can I get ye?" she smiled at us with a toothless grin.

"Er, nothing for me," Zoe cringed.

"Nor me," I added.

No way was I drinking out of a cup here – they were more disgusting than my gym kit after a whole year of not being washed!

"Me neither," Luke said to the barmaid.

"Please yerself," she huffed, turning to walk away.

"Actually," Luke shouted above the grunts and jeers at the bar, "my friends are looking for a ship that will sail into the Seismic Square."

It was as if someone had pressed a MUTE switch in the tavern. Suddenly, everyone stopped talking, music stopped playing, the cats and dogs stopped howling, and even the snoring man stopped snoring!

I looked around at the dirty faces in the room – their expressions ranged from shock to disgust to anger.

"Who speaks o' the Seismic Square?" boomed a deep voice from the back of the bar.

The crowd parted to reveal a tall, broad man

with a big red beard and a monkey on his shoulder. Both the man and the monkey had a patch over their left eyes. The man walked towards us, a heavy sword and a pouch of money hanging by his side.

"Who are you?" I asked him.

"I be Dan," he answered. "Dangerous Dan. And this 'ere be Swains," he pointed to the monkey on his shoulder.

"Hi, Dangerous Dan," I said back. Dangerous

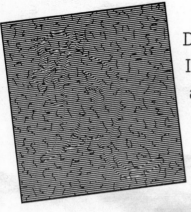

Dan was the biggest man I'd ever seen – practically a giant. A while ago I might have been scared of someone like that but I'd been on a few Adventures by now and seen far worse than a stinky pirate. I held out my hand to shake Dan's in greeting. His filthy fingers wrapped around mine, squeezing my hand until it hurt.

"I'm Will Solvit," I told him, pulling my hand away. "This is Zoe, and this is Captain Luke – he brought us here."

"'Tis a foolish man who brings two young'uns to the Port o' Lost Souls," Dan growled, squinting his good eye. "And a foolish young'un to speak o' things they know nothin' about."

"I do know about the Seismic Square,"
I replied, "and I know I need to go there."
Dangerous Dan might be huge and think he's
'dangerous' but he doesn't scare me – I've come
face-to-face with aliens, cannibals, dragons and
flesh-eating mummies!

"If you can't sail me to the Seismic Square then
I suggest you sit back down and stop wasting
my time," I continued. A loud jeer rose from the
crowd and a few people banged on the wooden
tables with their glasses, splashing sickly-
smelling rum all over the place.

"Ye know who 'e be, laddie?" the ugly
barmaid asked me with astonishment.

"Does he know who I am?" I retorted.

"Ye just a boy," Dangerous Dan laughed. "An'
I'm the biggest, baddest most ruthless pirate to
e'er sail the seven seas!"

39 Messy!

Zoe bravely stepped up beside me and said loudly, "For someone who's so bad and dangerous, you seem a bit scared of sailing into some stupid square!"

"Ne'er scared, lassie," he grinned at us with black teeth, "I just know that ye could nay afford the services o' me and my crew."

"Well, that's where you're wrong," replied Luke, stepping forwards and pulling out a small leather pouch from his pocket. He opened it up and a golden gleam shone onto his face. "How much do you want?"

"Well, that be a start," Dan said, snatching the gold from Luke's pouch.

"We be needin' that again when we return," said a loud voice from the back of the room. A small, blonde woman dressed like a man stormed towards us. She had a face full of dirt and freckles, curly hair and a huge curved sword at her side.

"Long-shot Laura," she introduced herself. "I be Dan's first mate an' the only lady pirate on the seas," she added proudly.

"Hi," I reached out my hand towards Long-shot Laura's. She spat into her palm and shook my hand with a grip stronger than Dangerous Dan's.

"Pleased to meet ye!" she grinned. "But before ye be boarding our ship, ye'll 'ave to pass a pirate test."

"A test?" Zoe and I repeated at the same time, quickly exchanging a worried glance.

"Ah, yes," Captain Luke sighed. "I should have warned you about this. Most pirates won't take you to sea unless you first pass a pirate test."

"Ye be walkin' the plank, fightin' the crocs and

livin' to tell the tale, me hearties!" Dangerous Dan grinned wickedly. "Ye ready?"

"Lead us to the plank!" I replied loudly.

Zoe's face drained of colour and she grabbed my arm.

"Will, what are you doing?" she whispered.

"Don't sweat it," I told her. "We'll be fine."

Long-shot Laura and Dangerous Dan led us out of Stinky Sal's Tavern. A whole bunch of rowdy pirates followed us to watch.

We walked around the back of the tavern to a large swamp. An old, shipwrecked boat was moored on the edge. Thrashing around in the murky water were dozens of hungry crocodiles.

"So, laddie," Long-shot Laura grinned, "all ye and yer lassie need be doin' is walkin' the plank of this 'ere ship, jumpin' in the waters and swimmin' out again. If ye live, then ye board our ship and we sail ye where'er ye need be."

"If ye fall," Dan growled, "the crocs are gonna 'ave ye for supper!"

Everyone started cheering. Even the monkey on Dan's shoulder jumped up and down, clapping his hands together.

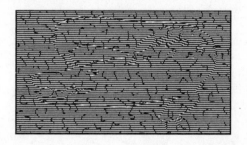

"Easy!" I shouted, silencing the crowd. "Just stick close to me," I whispered to Zoe. "I know what I'm doing."

"Good luck, Will," Captain Luke said, taking his hat off and saluting me.

Well done me hearties.

Zoe and I swam to the side of the swamp and clambered out.

The pirates congratulated us – we had passed the test! They led us back onto the beach.

There she be, The Pride of the Waterfront.

"That be the finest ship e'er built," Dan said, wading through the water towards the ship. "The Pride's seen some fierce battles and some wondrous booty – now she be sailin' into 'er greatest adventure yet."

I turned to Luke and shook his hand, "Thank you for taking us this far."

"I'll be here waiting for you when you return," he said. "Then I'll take you, your mother and Zoe to safe land."

"Thanks, Luke," I smiled, pleased that I had another Adventurer I could trust.

A small rope ladder swung from the side of the boat. Zoe and I followed Long-shot Laura and Dangerous Dan as we climbed up the ladder and onto the ship.

Luke was standing on the shore, waving at us.

"Good luck, young Adventurer," he called.

I was going to need it!

"Lug 'er out to sea!" Dangerous Dan screamed at the dozen men standing on the ship's deck. The men scattered and began to winch the boat's sails into the air and push the oars out into the water.

We waved back at Luke as The Pride of the Waterfront drifted out to sea. We were heading into the unknown – with nothing but pirates taking us there!

CHAPTER FOUR
ALL ABOARD

Girls' stuff! YUK!

Before my Adventure with pirates, I knew less about ships and sailing than I do about ballet. And trust me, I know less than nothing about ballet!

Long-shot Laura and Dangerous Dan quickly introduced us to the crew of The Pride of the Waterfront and the positions they held onboard the ship . . .

- **Captain = Dangerous Dan (he was in charge of everything)**
- **First mate = Long-shot Laura (the Captain's second-in-command)**

- Quartermaster = Deafenin' Don (he was in charge of the crew and VERY LOUD)
- Boatswain = Mad-eyed Mick (he kept the ship in top condition with his eagle eyes)
- Gunner = Gun-ho Hovis (he oversaw all the Pride's firearms and cannons)
- Powder monkey = Small Stan (a boy about six years old who did all the horrid jobs)
- Carpenter = Wooden-leg Lenny (he helped Mad-eyed Mick look after the ship)
- Doc = Dutch Doc (a doctor who only spoke in Dutch)
- Cook = Feed'em Fred (he cooked all the meals)
- Shanty boys = Moby and Toby (identical twins who helped Small Stan out with the jobs no one else wanted to do)

Long-shot Laura and Dangerous Dan's crew may have had different jobs and nicknames, but they all looked as rotten and unwashed as each other. They seemed to talk in half words and half grunts as they went about the ship, pulling the rigging, cooking up meals and telling jokes to pass the time at sea. But as far as pirates went, they all seemed friendly enough.

Moby and Toby showed me and Zoe below deck to where we would be sleeping during the voyage to the Seismic Square. The entire crew (even Dan and Laura) slept in hammocks that hung from rafters in the ship's hull. The swinging beds were surrounded by cages filled with clucking chickens, boxes of dynamite and bottles of rum. Rats ran over the dirty ship floor, eating up scraps that had been thrown at the chickens.

"Remind me why I thought it was a good idea

to come and help you with this Adventure?" said Zoe, looking at our new home in horror.

"Because this is my most important Adventure yet," I reminded her. "I'm here to rescue my mum – remember?"

We headed back up on deck. Dangerous Dan and Swains the monkey were waiting for us with Deafenin' Don, the Quartermaster.

"Ye ready for yer lesson in sailin'?" asked Dan.

"Huh?" I raised an eyebrow.

"Ye young'uns are pirates now. Ye be needin' to know 'ow to sail," he added, spitting onto the floor.

"I guess," I shrugged. Being able to captain a pirate ship was quite a cool thing to be taught.

Zoe and I sat down on a couple of upturned rum boxes and listened to Deafenin' Don explain (well, shout) about all the things pirates needed to know. Here's what he told us:

The parts of a ship:

- Bow – front of ship
- Aft – back of ship
- Rigging – ropes
- Topsail – the highest sail on the ship
- Mainsail – large sail below the topsail
- Rudder – large device at the back of the ship, which helps steer
- Hold – storage area below deck
- Mast – pole with sails on
- Hull – body of ship
- Port – left side of ship when facing the bow
- Starboard – right side of ship when facing the bow
- Anchor – large heavy weight that's lowered

Anchors away!

into the sea to hold the ship in place

Sailing in rough weather:

- Make sure all the rigging is tight
- Secure any loose items on deck
- Close the hatches so water can't get below deck
- Reduce speed

How to fire a cannon:

1. Cover the cannon's air vent
2. Insert a damp sponge into the barrel of the cannon to clear out debris
3. Place a charge down the barrel of the cannon and ram it to the bottom
4. Insert a cannon ball into the firearm

KABOOM!!

5. Carefully insert a fuse
6. Aim the cannon
7. Light the fuse, and run away

"Dinner be served, me hearties," shouted Feed'em Fred, the ship's cook. I'd been so busy listening to Deafenin' Don tell us about ships, I hadn't noticed how late it was getting. We'd been on the ship for hours – and I hadn't eaten anything for ages. My stomach let out a loud growl – I was starving.

Everyone sat down on deck and we were fed a stew that tasted kinda like chicken but smelt like mud. It was disgusting, a bazillion times worse than anything Grandpa Monty would cook.

"What is this?" Zoe asked suspiciously as the pirates gobbled down their rank dinner.

"Best not to ask," I told her.

"So," I said to Laura and Dan, eating the food carefully, "how did you get your nicknames?"

"I be the best long-distance gun shooter in these parts," said Laura, letting out a loud belch.

"And I be the most dangerous beast to e'er float 'pon the seas," Dan said, sucking on a chicken bone.

"Now ye tell us, young Will," Laura belched every word. "Why are ye askin' to be ta'en to the Seismic Square?"

"Heard of the Seismic Siren?" I asked.

A loud "AYE!" rang out from the crew.

"That's my mum," I told them quietly. "I'm going there to rescue her."

"Y'er brave, laddie," said Dan.

"I know a tale 'bout the Seismic Siren," piped up Small Stan, the tiny boy who was eating his stew off the floor.

"What?" I asked. "What did you hear about her?"

"Stand up, laddie," Dan said. "Tell a tale like the true pirate ye be."

Small Stan stood up and nervously shuffled into the circle of pirates sitting on the ship's deck. Mad-eyed Mick, the Boatswain, passed the small boy a flaming torch to hold. Small Stan held it up above his head so it shone on him as he spoke.

"Before me ma and pa be sellin' me to this 'ere ship, they be tellin' me the tale o' the Seismic Siren and the fortress she be kept in." He lowered his voice, as if he was telling us a secret. "Many years ago . . . a great big cat-like monster, with claws as sharp as swords and a bite as fierce as a shark, brought a lady to the Seismic Square. The monsters 'ad ta'en the lady away from loved ones to 'old 'er prisoner. They locked 'er in a castle that floats on an island in the middle o' the square. She be there for 'undreds of years . . . singin' to keep 'erself company and speakin' o' 'er family who she missed. The Siren be kept in a time vortex and can ne'er grow old or die so long as she be prisoner. The monsters 'ave put 'er there so that, one day, a brave adventurer be comin' and rescue 'er. But that adventurer be fallin' into their trap. For it is 'e, the rescuer, that they be wantin' – not the lady."

Silence rang out and the wind rattled in my ears.

It didn't take a genius to work out what was going on . . .

Huge, cat-like monsters = The Partek
Adventuring rescuer = me

Which means = The Partek had taken my mum to the Seismic Square to lure me into a trap.

"Will, what do you . . ." the sound of Zoe's voice was drowned out by a huge wave crashing over the side of the boat.

"All 'ands on deck!" Dangerous Dan screamed into the wind.

I looked up at the sky. It was rumbling with thunderous clouds and crackling with lightning. Waves as tall as Solvit Hall began to crash into the ship.

"This is it," I thought. "We're going to die."

CHAPTER FIVE
THE BEAST OF THE DEEP

Thank goodness Zoe and I had been given a lesson in how to work a ship.

As the vicious storm's waves lapped over the ship's sides, all I could think about (other than staying alive) was how grateful I was that I'd listened to Deafenin' Don when he taught us about boats.

Zoe and I climbed up the rigging and helped Moby and Toby tighten the sails. Then, remembering everything we'd learned, we helped the crew take whatever we could below deck and closed all the hatches to stop the water getting into the ship's hull.

The waves continued to rise and gush around

the ship, soaking everything on board. Everyone grabbed whatever they could find to scoop out the water filling up the ship – if we hadn't, then we would have sunk for sure.

Just when I thought the storm was calming down, a huge shape started to rise out of the water. It looked like a giant sea serpent. Its eyes glowed in the dark night and the moonlight reflected off of its scaly body.

The sea serpent let out a roar that sounded like the wailing of a great blue whale and the screeching of a dying cat – it was awful.

"Fight to the death!" Long-shot Laura screamed at us. She threw a sword towards me. "Ye bring us 'ere, laddie," she shouted. "Now ye save us!"

I felt a heavy hand shove me from behind and push me forwards, towards the side of the ship that the sea beast was gliding towards.

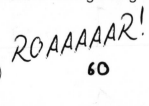

ROAAAAAR!

60

I gulped hard.

My Adventure tools were below deck, so all I had was the sword Long-shot Laura had given me. Luckily, thanks to the training I've had with knights, samurai warriors and the Roman army, I'm awesome with a sword.

The beast roared at me and its head rose above the side of the ship, revealing at least five rows of razor-sharp teeth in the top and bottom of its mouth.

I bravely climbed onto the side of the ship as the waves lapped at my feet and the boat rocked violently beneath me.

"Come here and meet your death, beast!" I screamed into the wind.

The sea beast rose higher into the air and opened its mouth wide, howling loudly.

The serpent's heavy head lunged towards me. I

held out my sword, hoping to stop it before it had the chance to eat me.

The beast's sharp jaws closed in on me. I was about to plunge my blade deep into his scaly throat when I noticed two things:

1. the terror in the beast's eyes
2. a white envelope between its teeth

Without thinking, I jumped into the air and reached for the envelope between the beast's teeth. My feet landed back on the slippery ship's side, and before I could have a swipe at the beast it had disappeared back below the crashing waves.

"Will!" Zoe shouted, pulling me down from the side of the ship and back onto the deck. "Are you OK?"

"Yeah," I answered, bewildered by what had just happened. "I don't think the sea beast came to hurt us. I think it came to give me this."

I held up the white envelope with my name, Will Solvit, clearly written on the front.

"What?" Zoe looked as confused as I felt.

"Hurrah for the laddie!" shouted Dangerous Dan, running over the deck towards me with Swains the monkey skidding on the wet deck behind him.

"All souls below deck for more stew," shouted Feed'em Fred the cook.

Long-shot Laura swung her arm around me and squeezed my shoulder hard.

"Well done, laddie," she said.

Zoe and I followed the pirates below deck into the stinky, dark hull.

"Keep them busy for a sec," I whispered to Zoe. "I need to read my letter."

She nodded and caught up with the rest of the crew as they headed below deck.

I snuck off into a corner and ripped open the envelope.

A letter in the jaws of a sea beast was definitely the strangest place I've received one yet!

WILL'S FACT FILE

Ahoy there, matey,

All ye cowardly landlubbers probably love a good pirate yarn, full of swashbuckling heroes swinging from rigging and talking in strange pirate slang. But how much do you know about real pirates? Did you know that the Queen of England encouraged pirates to plunder Spanish treasure ships? And did you know that any victim resisting capture would be ruthlessly butchered by pirates?

Read on to discover a treasure trove of info about those dastardly rogues who menaced the high seas in ages of old.

Timeline

1300 BC
Phoenician pirates attack the coasts around Ancient Egypt.

75 BC
A motley crew of Cilician pirates hold Julius Caesar ransom.

1243
Henry III of England is one of the first to give a letter of marque (a pirate's licence).

1400s
Corsairs terrorize the seas around North Africa until the 18th century.

1587
On the orders of Queen Elizabeth I, Sir Francis Drake destroys a Spanish fleet at Cadiz.

1600s
King James I of England withdraws all pirate licences.

1650–1720
Sometimes called the Golden Age of Piracy.

1716
Blackbeard and his men terri sailors on the Atlantic Ocean and Caribbean Sea.

1719
Anne Bonny joins Calico Jack's crew and becomes one of the most famous female pirates of the Caribbean.

1856
Seafaring nations join together to ban piracy.

Pirates:

- were seafaring thieves.
- were usually brutal scoundrels.
- flew the Jolly Roger as an invitation for ships to surrender.
- normally attacked ships but sometimes targeted coastal towns.
- were sometimes called buccaneers or corsairs.
- sometimes operated under a licence given by their government.
- were sometimes disgruntled seamen seeking their fortune.
- were lured to their lawless life by the promise of making a fast buck.
- still exist in some parts of the world today.

Cilician pirates captured Julius Caesar when he sailed to Greece.

Pirates of old

Pirates have existed since ancient times.

- Phoenician pirates attacked Ancient Egypt.
- Pirates attacked prosperous trading ships from Ancient Greece.
- Piracy was encouraged by some senators to satisfy the demand for slaves in Ancient Rome.

Privateers

Privateers were legal pirates according to the government that they shared their ill-gotten gains with.

- They captured cargoes and enemy vessels.
- Sir Francis Drake was a privateer who preyed on Spanish ships.
- He was a hero to Queen Elizabeth I and a villain to the King of Spain.

Privateers had a licence to attack and steal from enemy ships.

Corsairs

Corsairs made swift attacks in sleek, oar-powered galleys.

- Corsairs were also known as Barbary Pirates because they prowled the Barbary Coast.
- The most famous corsairs were the Barbarossa Brothers.
- The super-fast galleys were rowed by up to 90 slaves. Some were captured sailors.

The corsairs seized sailors and passengers to sell as slaves.

Brutal buccaneers

Buccaneers replaced the privateers when pirate licences were withdrawn.

- English, Dutch and French outlaws, slaves and adventurers joined together to attack Spanish shipping.
- Spanish colonies were raided and men, women and children killed.
- Buccaneers dressed in uncured animal hides and stank of blood.

François L'Ollonais cut flesh off his prisoners till their eyes popped out.

These pirates boasted of their exploits around the Caribbean.

The Golden Age

From 1650 to 1720 privateers relieved ships of their goods on the Caribbean and Atlantic coast of North America.

- This period is sometimes referred to as the Golden Age of Piracy.
- As peace fell on most of Europe, pirate numbers increased with privateers and seamen out of work.
- The most famous pirate of the Golden Age was Blackbeard.

Blackbeard

Blackbeard was probably the most feared pirate to sail the seven seas.

- He cultivated a wild, bloodthirsty reputation that made many victims surrender without putting up a fight.
- He slung pistols, cutlasses and daggers across his huge chest.
- His real name was Edward Teach.
- He was killed by the Royal Navy.

Blackbeard had wild eyes, a black beard and lit fuses on his hat.

Other famous pirates

Some pirates were folk heroes among ordinary people.

- Henry Morgan, a brutal buccaneer, won an English knighthood.
- Black Bart captured more ships than Blackbeard.
- Calico Jack had two of the most notorious female pirates of all time in his crew.

Henry Evans, a pirate captain, managed to retire before capture.

Female pirates

Most pirates were men but there were some female pirates.

- Mary Read disguised herself as a man to join Calico Jack's crew.
- Grace O'Malley from Ireland was a fearless pirate captain.
- Anne Dieu-le-Veut was a ruthless French pirate who fought alongside her husband.

Anne Bonny, a famous female pirate, sailed with Calico Jack.

Attack

Pirates generally managed to get their prize without too much bloodshed.

- They used small, speedy ships that could hide in secret coves.
- They used grappling hooks to pull target ships close enough to board.
- They would board the ship and deal swiftly and violently with anyone who tried to fight them.

Pirates would shout and fire pistols in a terrifying manner.

Life at sea

A pirate's life wasn't all fun and fighting on the high seas.

- Days might be spent mending sails and splicing ropes.
- When fresh supplies ran out, hard tack (rock-hard biscuits, often full of bugs) was the only food.
- Every pirate ship would have a supply of grog (rum mixed with water).

Food and water were scarce and rats were plentiful.

Loot was divided up and the captain often had the biggest share.

Pirate code

Pirate crews had strict codes of conduct that gave some order and stability.

- Rules were drawn up and agreed upon before a voyage.
- Weapons had to be clean and ready to use at all times.
- Gambling onboard was forbidden.
- Smuggling a woman aboard the ship was strictly against the rules.

Piratical punishment

Pirates who broke their own set of rules were tried and punished by their fellow shipmates.

- An offender would receive 40 lashes with nine strands of knotted rope for hitting a fellow shipmate.
- They'd walk the plank blindfolded if they double-crossed the captain.
- Culprits could be tossed overboard.

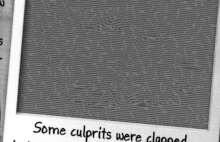

Some culprits were clapped in irons and chucked into the hold.

A grisly end

From around 1830 governments began to take a tough stand against pirates.

· Naval captains were ordered to capture pirates dead or alive.
· Some corpses of executed pirates were hung in chains as a warning to others.
· Captured pirates saw out their years in disease-ridden prisons.
· Others retired avoiding capture.

William Kidd was tarred and hung in a cage on the Thames River.

Pirate talk

Pirates developed a language all of their own while at sea. Here are some examples:

· ahoy — hello
· booty — treasure
· grog — a pirate's favourite drink
· landlubber — non-sailor
· me hearty — friend
· shiver me timbers — golly gosh

Try writing a letter about pirates, using pirate language, to a friend.

Pirate films

Pirates make great characters for swashbuckling movies and novels.

· Treasure Island's Long John Silver is used as a pirate template by writers.
· Errol Flynn swung from the rigging in the classic Captain Blood.
· The Pirates of the Caribbean movies star Johnny Depp.
· Captain Hook is loosely based on the real Blackbeard.

Treasure Island is a tale about pirates and buried treasure.

CHAPTER SIX
A PIRATE'S LIFE FOR ME!

WHAT DO SEA MONSTERS HAVE FOR DINNER?

FISH AND SHIPS!

WILL, YOUR BRAVERY IN THE FACE OF DANGER IS ASTOUNDING. YOU SHOULD BE TRULY PROUD OF YOURSELF. YOU'RE BECOMING THE ADVENTURER YOU NEED TO BE TO RESCUE YOUR PARENTS AND FACE THE DEADLY BATTLES AHEAD.

WHEN YOU ARRIVE IN THE SEISMIC SQUARE, YOU WILL HAVE TO FACE THREE CHALLENGES BEFORE YOU FIND YOUR MOTHER:

THE FIRST IS SOFTER THAN RAIN AND FALLS
FROM THE SKY.
THE SECOND IS A FEAR YOU ARE ~~GOING~~ TO DIE.
THE THIRD IS IN DARKNESS, YOU WILL LOSE YOUR WAY.
SHE'LL BE WAITING FOR YOU AT THE END OF
YOUR STAY.

THE CLUE IN CAPTAIN LUKE'S LETTER -
THAT HE WOULD MEET ME ONE DAY - IS RIGHT.
BUT YOU, WILL - YOU'VE ALREADY MET ME . . .

We were at sea for what felt like months before
we even came close to the Seismic Square, which
was a good thing cuz I needed all that time to
figure out the clues in my letter.

"Something 'softer than rain and falls from
the sky' could be snow," said Zoe as we helped

Mad-eyed Mick the Boatswain tighten the boat's rigging one day. "I can't think what else it could be."

"Not much snow round these parts," said Mad-eyed Mick, sitting down on an empty, upturned rum box to rest. "These 'ere be the warmest waters o' the seven seas."

"He's right," I said to Zoe, wiping the sweat from my forehead (it was horribly hot and I couldn't remember the last time I had taken a shower). "I can't imagine it snowing when it's as warm as this."

"Well I don't see what else falls from the sky that's softer than rain," she said irritably.

I kept reminding Zoe that I'd make sure Morph time travelled back to the exact moment we'd left home as soon as we found Mum. But I think Zoe was worried that Morph wouldn't do that – she was way more concerned about missing school than I was. Who needs school when you have pirates to teach you about ships?

One evening, Zoe and I were sitting up on deck after dinner, watching the endless horizon bob about in the distance when she said, "And what about your second clue?"

"What about it?" I asked, watching a gull circle above our boat, The Pride of the Waterfront, looking for food scraps to swoop down upon.

"A fear that you're going to die," she said. "That sounds really awful."

"Look," I told her, "I have no idea what the clues in the letter mean. But I don't see the point of worrying about what we might find – we've just got to be prepared to face the worst."

"How can we prepare for what's ahead?" Zoe replied angrily. "We've been stuck at sea for

Dry crackers again?! ☹

months!"

So far, we'd passed our time on the ship by being taught the ways of pirates.

Every day we'd learn something new. We'd wake up in the morning and Feed'em Fred would make us breakfast (usually just dry crackers and water), then we'd spend the day learning how to sail and fight, and speak like a pirate. We also discovered how to navigate at sea.

One evening Dangerous Dan taught us a famous pirate sea shanty. You have to sing it with your sword in your hand as you stand in a circle with your fellow crew members. These are the lyrics . . .

T' me, yo-ho-ho,
A pirate's life for me, for me!
That time in evenin' when men need deceivin',

Me soft patch covers me eye,
I'm proud of me peg leg,
me grog and me ale keg,
We're buccaneers till we die!

Hope Mum doesn't know this!

One day Laura taught me one of the greatest
pirate tricks ever – how to tell if someone's lying!

"See Feed'em Fred's eye twitch and the way
'e clenches 'is fist when 'e speaks," she said,
pointing to the pirate, "'e be lying. There be
more stew left for us." She was right, Feed'em
Fred was telling fibs – he wanted the rest of the
stew for himself, so he told us it was empty!

After weeks at sea, the pirates trusted Zoe and
me completely. It was if we'd always been a part
of the crew.

"I be teachin' ye somethin' I don't teach
many," Dangerous Dan said one day. "I be

teachin' ye 'ow to speak to monkeys."

He wasn't lying – he didn't clench his fists or twitch his eyes. Dangerous Dan taught us how to talk like monkeys but he made us promise not to tell a soul (sorry).

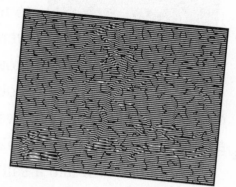

Soon, Zoe and I didn't care that it was baking hot or that we hadn't showered in ages, or that all we were eating was chicken stew. Sleeping in hammocks suddenly felt like the most comfortable thing in the world and sharing the hull with the chickens and rats seemed like fun.

I was getting used to the life of a pirate – and I was loving it!

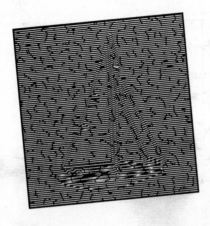

Zoe was beginning to feel the same.

"When we're back home, Will," she said to me one day, as we were sitting in the crow's nest (that's a lookout tower at the top of the large mast), "I think we should get a boat and sail it around at the weekends."

"Morph can turn into a sailboat," I told her.

"Awesome," she grinned at me (her teeth were starting to look a bit yellow).

"Hey, Zoe," I grinned back, "why does it take pirates so long to learn the alphabet?"

"Dunno," she replied.

"Cuz they spend years at C!"

We both cracked up with laughter and

drummed our dirty hands on the crow's nest floor at my joke.

I noticed Zoe had stopped laughing. I glanced at her and her face had frozen over with terror.

I traced her gaze towards the horizon and instantly shot to my feet.

There, in the distance, I could see a swirling whirl of white mist. It looked like a snow storm on top of the ocean.

"Impossible," I muttered.

"We've arrived at the Seismic Square," Zoe said gravely. "Sound the alarm!"

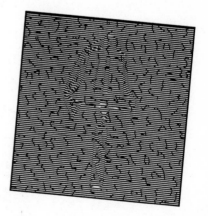

I grabbed the handle of a large bell in the crow's nest and started ringing it with all my strength.

"All hands on deck," Zoe called down below. "Storm ahead!"

We climbed over the side of the crow's nest and grabbed onto nearby rigging. We both slid down the ropes and back onto the deck of the ship.

This was it, we'd finally arrived at the place my mother was being kept prisoner.

And I'd have to pass my first challenge.

Yikes, rough weather ahead!

CHAPTER SEVEN
LAND AHOY!

The whirling white mist looked like an angry tornado tearing up the sea. And we were heading right towards it!

"This is it, Will," Zoe screamed at me as every pirate on board began to frantically run around the deck. "This is what we came here to do, what we've waited months at sea for – this is the beginning of the end. You're going to find your mum!"

She was right.

This was the beginning of the end – we were heading straight into the Seismic Square – where

I'd find my mum. But I knew I had a difficult journey ahead and finding her wouldn't be easy.

"Shimmy up the timbers," Long-shot Laura called at Moby and Toby. The two small boys climbed up the tall sail masts and started pulling on the rigging and sails to steady the ship.

"Hands on the cannons!" Gun-ho Hovis screamed into the wind. Mad-eyed Mick and Deafenin' Don ran towards the sides of the ship and began to stuff the cannons with gunpowder and aim them at the swirling mist in the distance.

Dangerous Dan and Long-shot Laura took their places at the helm of the ship. Dan had his hands on the large steering wheel and shouted war threats into the wind, warding off whatever lay ahead. "Arrrrrr, be gone with you, arrrrrr!"

Swains the monkey stood tall on Laura's shoulder, as if he was ready to leap into the enemy and tear them apart.

"Swabbies," Laura called to me and Zoe. We ran over to the front of the ship. "I know not what lies ahead. 'Tis nothin' like I've seen before. Prepare for battle, prepare to fight, prepare to die!"

Armed with swords and knives, Zoe and I stood proud, ready for the battle to begin.

Suddenly, the air around us became heavy and wet — as if we were sailing into a rainstorm.

"It's snow!" shouted Zoe. "Only it's not cold, like normal snow. It feels warm."

Soon there was nothing around us but swirling white mist. Zoe was right, the snow wasn't cold but it was wet and soaked me to the bone. All I could see was white mist, I couldn't see Zoe, Laura, Dan or any of the other pirates. I couldn't even see my own hand if I held it up to my face.

I took a deep breath and coughed out a load of water I'd inhaled. This was my first test, and I knew how to pass it!

"Everyone below deck!" I screamed into the wind. "This is my battle! I'll steer The Pride of the Waterfront through this storm!"

"All souls below deck!" I heard Long-shot Laura call.

The sounds of shuffling feet and muffled voices

filled my ears as everyone made their way to the galley below deck.

A strong hand gripped my arm.

"Arrr, laddie," said Dan's voice. "I be the captain of this 'ere ship and I nay be lettin' 'er go into this storm alone."

"OK," I agreed.

Having Dan there wasn't exactly my plan, but I knew how important it was for a captain to stay with his ship.

I reached into my Adventure bag and pulled out the night vision goggles.

"Hold onto me," I called to Dan, putting the goggles over my head.

Result – they worked! I could see clearly through the mist and snow.

The water was surprisingly calm beneath the manic tornado-like swirl of white mist.

They totally ROCK!

I stepped up to the helm of the boat and held on to the steering wheel.

"I can see where we're going," I reassured Dan. "I'll steer us through this mist, don't worry!"

The wheel was heavy. It took all my weight to move it from left to right, but I kept the ship on course, dodging any rough waves.

Eventually the mist became lighter, and I could see beyond it, to clear skies and land.

"We're nearly out of the mist!" I shouted happily.

"We be making a pirate out of ye yet, laddie," Dan congratulated me, squeezing my left shoulder so hard that it hurt.

"Go down and bring the others up on deck," I told him. "There's land approaching and my guess is that we're going to have to drop the anchors."

"Aye, aye," Dan agreed. He let go of my shoulder and I heard his footsteps fade away as he went below deck to fetch the others.

I'd done it. I'd used my Adventurer tools and skills to successfully pass my first challenge. If I hadn't, we'd all be fish-food below the sea now – for sure!

"Will!" Zoe cried, running towards me. "You did it!"

"The goggles," I told her.

"Of course," she smiled.

"Land ahoy! Land ahoy!" Small Stan shouted from the crow's nest.

"Prepare to travel 'arbour-bound and drop anchors!" Dangerous Dan instructed his crew.

Everyone knew what to do. Dangerous Dan and Long-shot Laura stood at the front of the ship, telescopes pressed to their eyes and their hands

resting on their swords.
Deafenin' Don,
Mad-eyed Mick and
Gun-ho Hovis all stood
by the cannons, ready
to shoot any enemies
waiting on shore.

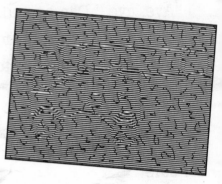

Small Stan stayed in the crow's
nest while Moby and Toby pulled at the rigging,
getting ready to moor. Everyone else got into
their positions, ready for what lay ahead.

"So what now?" Zoe wondered aloud.

"A fear that I'm going to die," I said, hearing
the terror in my own voice.

There were a gazillion things that could scare
me into thinking I was going to die: aliens,
monsters, guns, swords. But which one was I
going to have to face? I was about to find out!

CHAPTER EIGHT
THE SEISMIC SQUARE

The Pride of the Waterfront's anchors dropped into the sea.

"Stay 'ere and keep guard," Dangerous Dan instructed his crew. "Deafenin' Don, you're in charge until I get back."

"Aye, aye, Captain!" Don shouted back.

Moby and Toby lowered a smaller boat over the side of the Pride. Zoe, Laura, Dan and I all climbed into it and Long-shot Laura rowed us to shore. She was the strongest woman I'd ever seen. She didn't even flinch as she pulled her heavy oars through the water.

"Can ye believe it?" Long-shot Laura said to

Dan. "The stuff o' legends and 'ere we are, the Seismic Square."

"Aye," Dan agreed, squinting in the sunlight. "But will we e'er leave? No one else e'er 'as."

Everyone was silent.

When the water became shallow enough, we climbed out of the boat and waded towards the shore. There was nothing in sight, just trees and sand.

"Where do we go?" Zoe asked.

"How should I know?" I replied. "Why don't we just walk inland and see what we find?"

No one had any better ideas, so after dragging the boat onto the beach we all headed off towards the trees.

The island was hot and sticky. The trees were tall and blocked out the sunlight from the sky.

"Maybe this is the darkness the letter spoke

about?" Zoe said, pushing a large tree branch out of the way. "I can hardly see where I'm going."

"Here," I said, reaching into my bag. "Take one of these."

I passed an omnilume to Zoe and one to Dan and Laura.

"So 'ow do these work, young Will?" Dan said, looking confused.

"You snap them like this," I showed him. "And it lights up the darkness."

With four omnilumes between us we could just about see where we were going in the dark jungle. It was eerily quiet – no bugs or animal sounds. It was as if nothing lived there at all.

We walked for ages. Eventually I could see a clearing ahead. The sun was shining brightly into the clearing – the forest had been so dark I'd almost forgotten it was daytime. Then . . .

WHAT MONSTER CAN SIT ON THE END OF YOUR FINGER?

THE BOGEYMAN!

I BET YOU DIDN'T THINK YOU'D FIND YOURSELF IN A CASTLE AGAIN SO SOON. AT LEAST THIS ONE'S NOT HAUNTED - I PROMISE!

TURN ON YOUR COMPUTER - THERE'S SOMEONE WAITING TO SPEAK TO YOU.

"What's a computer?" asked Long-shot Laura, after I'd finished reading the letter out loud.

"Morph," I said, reaching into my bag and pulling out the miniature time machine. "I can turn Morph into a computer."

"Will," Zoe sighed. "You can't use the internet

here – we're in 1804, remember?"

"I've got to do what the letter tells me," I said confidently. I know it seems crazy – but weirder things have happened, trust me.

I quickly programmed Morph to transform into a computer. I placed the tiny time machine on the ground and stood back as it whizzed and whirred to life and sprung up as a laptop.

I opened it, logged onto the internet and cool – a signal.

"How is that happening?" Zoe gasped in shock.

"Who cares," I replied. "The important thing is that it's working."

Laura and Dan were speechless. They'd obviously never seen a computer before, let alone a time machine that turns into a computer!

Suddenly Morph's computer screen began to crackle and fill with static.

"Will Solvit," boomed a voice from inside my computer.

The static on the screen started to form a shape – the face of a cat-like creature.

The Partek!

"What do you want?" I shouted at my computer screen.

"We want you, Will Solvit, and we want you alive," replied the Partek from inside my computer.

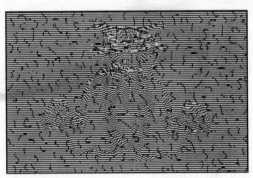

"Why?" I shouted back. "Why me?"

"You're special," it replied. "So special and you don't understand why."

"How do I rescue my mum?" I asked quickly.

"There's a hidden door in the walls of this room. You must walk through this door if you wish to find your mother."

"Where's the door?" Zoe asked, hovering over me. "How do we get it to open?"

"Will Solvit," growled the voice. "There's a riddle you must solve. To open the door, push the stone that has the answer to the riddle engraved upon it. The stone that you must push is on the ceiling."

I looked upwards; the ceiling was made of stone bricks – just like the walls. I could just about see that three of the stones had symbols engraved upon them.

"Listen carefully," boomed the voice from

my computer. "What runs but never walks, has a mouth but never talks, has a head but never weeps and has a bed but never sleeps?"

"How do I get up to the ceiling?" I asked.

Morph's computer screen suddenly went blank. The Partek had gone.

I felt something wet hit the top of my head.

"Arrrr!" screamed Dan, Laura and Zoe at once.

I looked up – water was gushing into the room through cracks in the ceiling.

As I deactivated Morph and put it back in my backpack, the water began to fill the room.

It was soon at ankle height, then up to our knees. The skeletons around us began floating in the water.

"Now we know how all these people died," Zoe shouted, beginning to panic. "The riddle, Will. We have to solve the riddle."

By now the water was nearly up to my neck. I was holding my backpack high above my head – trying to keep it dry. If Morph got wet it would short circuit and we would never get home!

"I can't even remember the riddle!" I shouted.

Dan and Laura were flapping wildly beside me.

"Swim," I told them. "Otherwise you'll drown."

"We can't swim!" Dan shouted at me with fear in his one eye. "We never learnt."

"Will, the riddle," Zoe reminded me. The water was bringing us closer to the ceiling and I could see the symbols on the three stone bricks.

One symbol looked like a star, one looked like waves and the other was in the shape of a square.

"What runs but never walks, has a mouth but never talks, has a head but never weeps and has

93

a bed but never sleeps?" Zoe repeated the riddle.

"I don't know!" I shouted, desperately trying to keep my head above the water. Dan and Laura were slipping below the water's surface – they were going to drown!

"It can't be a star," I shouted loudly. "A star doesn't have a mouth and it can't run."

"Neither can a square," Zoe replied.

"So it must be the other symbol I have to press – the symbol that looks like water."

"A river!" Zoe screamed. I looked over at her. We were inches from the ceiling and running out of air to breathe. Dan and Laura were nowhere to be seen – they'd slipped below the water.

"A river runs but never walks, has a mouth but never talks, has a head but never weeps and has a bed but never sleeps!" she shouted.

I quickly reached up and hit the stone brick

with a water symbol on it.

Suddenly the water began to disappear – as if it was seeping through the cracks in the floor below us.

Within moments we were back on the ground, dripping wet. Dan and Laura were madly coughing next to me.

"I thought we be gonners," Laura croaked, spitting out a mouthful of water.

I heard a loud click behind me.

A door had opened in the stone wall.

"What are we waiting for," Zoe smiled at me, picking herself off the floor and ringing out her clothes.

I stood up and helped Dan and Laura to their feet.

"Let's go!" I smiled back.

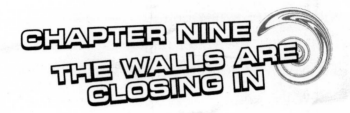

CHAPTER NINE
THE WALLS ARE CLOSING IN

The secret door in the wall led into a dark tunnel.
Water dripped from our clothes as I led Zoe,
Long-shot Laura and Dangerous Dan through the
dark and cold tunnel. All I could hear was the
sound of our footsteps and our dripping clothes
echoing on the stone floor.

"Where is this leadin'?" said Long-shot Laura.

"Back to shore I hope!" snorted Dan – he was
still mad from nearly being drowned.

"We're not going back without finding my mum
first," I told them. I'd come this far, there was no

way I was giving up now.

"But, Will," said Zoe, in a nervous voice. "You still have one more test to pass."

"'The third is in darkness, you will lose your way'," I whispered, remembering the clues in my letter.

Well, it was certainly dark in the tunnel. I couldn't see a thing! Even worse, we had accidentally left the omnilumes in the other room.

"Did you bring any more omnilumes with you?" asked Zoe.

"No," I said, annoyed with myself.

WHAM!!!

My face smashed against the stone wall – hard.

"Ouch!" Zoe screamed as she slammed into me from behind.

"Barnacles!" Dan cried as he crashed into Laura who fell into Zoe.

I put my hand out to push myself away
but there was nothing there – the wall had
disappeared.

SLAM!! CRASH!!

Something hard whacked into me from the
right and knocked me to the ground. Zoe, Laura
and Dan fell over at the same time.

"What is going on?" I shouted, picking myself
up from the floor.

"The walls are moving!" cried Zoe.

The loud sound of grinding stone filled my
ears as the wall on my left bashed into me and
knocked me to the ground.

"Arrrrrr!" Laura and Dan shouted in unison.

"Quick," I shouted, trying to run ahead.

"We're in a pitch-black maze with moving
walls!" Zoe shouted back, running up behind me.

SLAM!!! CRASH!!!

Once again, I ran into the stone wall – or the stone wall ran into me!

"What is going on?" Zoe screamed with fright.

Suddenly, I felt the amulet around my neck begin to get warm. The amulet has been translating for me ever since I found it in one of my letters.

"Can you hear that?" Laura whispered, her voice trembling with fear.

"Sounds like the call o' sirens, singin' sailors to their graves," Dan's voice trembled. You didn't have to be able to see his face to tell how scared he was. Clearly, moving walls and ghostly voices were one danger that Dangerous Dan had never come across before.

"The voices are getting louder." I felt Zoe's hand reach for me in the darkness and firmly grip my arm.

She was right, the voices were getting louder.

They sounded like a hundred people wailing in pain. It was horrible.

I felt my amulet get hotter and hotter, and suddenly the wails became words.

The amulet was helping me understand what the voices were saying:

"We guard the Seismic Siren," said the voices. "We will stay here until the end of time. Only the Master of Time, the worthy one, can pass."

"That's me!" I shouted. "I'm the Master of Time!"

"Will," Zoe shouted. "What are you talking

about?"

"Can't you hear that?" I said.

"What, the wailing?" she replied in the darkness.

"It's not wailing," I told her. "At least, not to me. The amulet is translating the voices for me."

"What are the voices saying?" she asked urgently.

"They're here to protect my mum until the end of time. The only person who can pass is me, the Master of Time."

"Step left," said the voices.

"Step left!" I instructed. Everyone took a sharp step to the left as the stone wall moved towards us from the right.

"Shiver me timbers!" sighed Dan. "How did you know that was coming?"

"The voices are telling me what to do," I said – realizing what was going on. "I can understand them. They're warning us what's coming next."

"Forwards, quickly!" wailed the ghostly voices.

"Move forwards – quick!" I told everyone.

We ran in front as the walls chased us from behind.

"Keep moving," the voices continued.

"Carry on," I instructed.

We walked further and further in the darkness. I listened carefully as the ghostly voices told me to step left, right, forwards or backwards. We did as they said and narrowly escaped being crushed by the heavy stone walls.

Slowly, the darkness started to lighten.

At first the brightness stung my eyes – I'd been so used to the pitch black, it felt weird to see again. Finally, everything came into focus.

"They keep me tied to this chair," Mum said sadly.

"Who's they?" asked Long-shot Laura suspiciously.

"Oh, Mum, this is Long-shot Laura and Dangerous Dan," I explained. "They're pirates. They brought me here to rescue you."

Mum's face tightened at the words 'pirates'.

"It's OK, Mum," I reassured her. "I'm used to being an Adventurer these days. I can handle a couple of pirates, no problem."

"Oh, I'm so proud of you," she said, as tears began to fall down her face.

"Mum, don't cry," I said, feeling uncomfortable. "I'm gonna bust you out of here. What do I need to do?"

"You need to give an answer to a riddle," she said, looking me in the eye.

"What riddle?"

Mum took a deep breath and stared at me intensely, "You're in a dark tunnel – it's pitch black," she said. "You have one match and one match only. You're also carrying a newspaper, a lamp and a candle. Which do you light first?"

"OK, let's think about this carefully," I said, concentrating.

"It's easy!" Zoe exclaimed.

"Don't sound easy t'me," said Laura, looking confused.

"'Tis the lamp," Dan said certainly. "It be lightin' the way for ye down the tunnel."

"No," said Zoe sternly. "Will, think about it."

"The answer must come from you, Will, and no one else. We can't help you," Mum explained.

I thought hard. I had no choice but to get it right.

Then the answer suddenly seemed obvious.
What did I light first?

"The match!" I said proudly.

There was a loud clank as Mum's metal chains fell to the floor.

She was free.

Zoe's not the
only clever one!

CHAPTER TEN
MRS SOLVIT

I hadn't kept track of when I last saw my mum, but it must have been months ago. We had travelled back in time to a prehistoric jungle to see dinosaurs. Only things hadn't exactly gone to plan and I'd ended up travelling back home and leaving Mum and Dad there. For ages I hadn't known if they were alive or dead. It turns out that somehow they'd been able to travel through time themselves. Then they'd become separated and Mum had ended up in the Seismic Square and Dad ended up who-knows-where.

I'd imagined meeting up with Mum a million times in my head, and never once had I thought about not showering for months before! But now that I'd finally found her I couldn't be less concerned about that. I was just mega-happy!

Mum threw her arms round me and squeezed me so hard I couldn't breathe.

"We have to get out of here," she whispered in my ear. "Before they come back."

"Before who come back? The Partek?" I asked.

"They've left," Mum said. "But they'll come back soon." She started walking off, back towards the tunnel that we'd walked through. "Quickly."

"We headin' back to shore?" Long-shot Laura asked.

"Back to The Pride of the Waterfront?" Dan added.

"Yeah, quickly," I answered. "Before the Partek come back."

I led everyone back through the pitch-black

tunnel with the moving walls. I listened to the instructions given to me by the voices in the darkness. We moved left, right, forwards and backwards, avoiding being squashed by the moving walls as we went.

Soon we came out into the stone room that we'd nearly drowned in. We stepped over the skeletons and ran through the castle. The door that we'd come through was open, and we ran out into the open air.

When we got back to the dark jungle, I wished I'd brought more omnilumes with me. I'm taking loads on my next Adventure.

I led the way, holding Mum's hand. Mum held Zoe's hand, Zoe held Laura's and Laura held Dan's. Travelling in a long line, we wound through the jungle in the darkness.

Eventually we made it back to the beach.

"Is that the pirate ship?" Mum asked, pointing to The Pride of the Waterfront in the distance.

"Yep," I smiled, "the ship that'll take us home."

Dan and Laura ran towards the small boat moored on the beach, ready to row us back to The Pride of the Waterfront. Zoe followed them.

Mum turned to me and took my face in her hands. I always hated it when she did that – but right then, I didn't care. I was just so pleased to have her

back again, at last.

"I'm so, so proud of you, Will," she said. "You've become an Adventurer. You've grown into a brave, strong and clever boy. I always knew you'd never let the family down."

"Hey, I'm a Solvit," I grinned up at her. "I'm just doing my job."

She bent down and gave me another huge hug.

"Look, Mum," I said. "I'm really pleased to see you, but we're about to get on a pirate ship – you've gotta quit the hugging, it's just not cool."

"OK," she said, pulling away from me.

"Come on, Will!" Zoe called over.

"Your friend Zoe is very pretty," Mum said.

"MUM!" I squirmed, turning bright red. She's so MEGA-embarrassing sometimes!

I introduced Mum to all of the crew as soon as we were on board The Pride of the Waterfront.

Aaaarrrgh! NO WAY!!!

We set sail back to the mainland. Everyone, apart from Dan and me, went below deck when we had to navigate through the thick white mist that we'd battled through on our way in.

"Ye be a fine pirate, laddie," Dangerous Dan said as the white mist thinned and we could see again.

"Thanks," I smiled. "Always good to know."

We spent the next few months at sea.

Mum seemed to love being on board a pirate ship. She helped Feed'em Fred with the cooking, taught Small Stan how to read and even taught Long-shot Laura how to make make-up out of fire ash, spit and beetroot juice.

I spent ages just talking to Mum. I told her all about my Adventures – about finding out that Grandpa Monty was a spy and how to use the amulet. I told her about going back to ancient

Egypt, Rome and the Aztecs. I told her about going into the future and about Dr Demonax and how I could use Morph to do loads of cool things. I missed out the parts in my stories that I knew Mum would hate – like battling zombie mummies and gladiators.

Mum told me all about what had happened to her since I last saw her.

"Your father and I lived in the jungle for a while," she said. "Henry knew that you wouldn't be able to return to us. So he spent his time inventing a new time machine. He used dinosaur dung, berries, rain water and lightning to forge a machine that would take us far enough into the future to meet other humans."

"Cavemen?" I asked, remembering the cave paintings I'd seen when I'd visited the Stone Age.

"Yes," she smiled. "We stayed there for a

while, until your father was able to modify the time machine to take us further into the future."

She became sad as she told the story.

"But our machine was stopped in time," she said sadly. "We were brought to a halt by horrible beasts. Cat-like creatures with claws for tongues and eyes like fire."

"The Partek," I said.

"They took me to the Seismic Square and trapped me in a time vortex. I was there for what felt like years and years. Only time didn't pass for me, I didn't age and every day felt like an eternity. I thought I'd never leave."

"Where did they take Dad?" I asked.

"I don't know," Mum replied. "They just took him away. They kept me in the Seismic Square, hoping that one day you'd come for me. Then one day they left. They said they had a better plan to capture you. They didn't care whether you rescued me or not – they'd have you in the end."

"Why do they want me so badly?" I asked, hoping Mum had an answer.

"Will," she said seriously, "you're brave and strong, but not yet strong enough to know the truth. But you'll find out when you're ready."

Great – I'd gone to all the trouble of saving my mum from a time vortex and she couldn't even tell me the truth! Mega-annoying!

At last, after what felt like ages at sea, I could just about make out the Port of Lost Souls on the horizon.

"Land ahoy!" called Mad-eyed Mick.

Then I heard a loud foghorn in the sky. We

all looked up and flying above us was Captain Luke's airship, The Godfather.

Captain Luke was waving at us from the metal basket. We all waved back.

"All hands on deck!" cried Long-shot Laura. "Pull the rigging, bring down the mainsail and get the anchor ready – we're coming in to harbour."

Pulling on the rigging felt like second nature to me after so long at sea.

Dangerous Dan was right – I would make an awesome pirate.

Captain Luke!

CHAPTER ELEVEN
MISSING PIECE OF THE PUZZLE

"Remember, laddie," Dangerous Dan beamed at me with black teeth as we came ashore, "ye an' the lassie Zoe can come back to the Pride whene'er you want."

"Thanks," I grinned back.

"We be proud to 'ave ye aboard," Long-shot Laura said as she shook my hand.

Zoe, Mum and I said goodbye to all the pirates and Swains the monkey.

We climbed into Captain Luke's airship, which had since landed, and waved to everyone on the ground as we lifted up into the air.

"So, young Adventurer," Captain Luke began as he steered The Godfather further into the sky, "you're one of the first to have travelled into the Seismic Square and lived to tell the tale. How does it feel?"

"Amazing!" smiled Zoe.

"It feels better than amazing," I added, looking over at Mum. "It's the best Adventure I've ever had."

"Thank you very much for looking after Will when he arrived here," Mum told Luke.

"Not a problem, Ma'am," he replied. "Young Will doesn't need much looking after."

Captain Luke flew us back to where he'd met us. The Godfather lowered to the ground and we all climbed out.

"Young Will," Luke said, taking me by the shoulder and walking me away from Mum and Zoe, "I need to speak to you in private, Adventurer-to-Adventurer."

"Of course," I said, lowering my voice.

"I had another letter," he said quietly. "It said that you'll be back here soon, needing my services again. The letter said that you're about to have your most dangerous Adventure yet."

A shudder ran down my spine.

"I just want you to know," Luke continued, "that I will follow you into any battle until the bitter end, you have my word."

"Thank you, Luke," I said, shaking his hand.

"Come on, Will," Mum called. "Let's go home."

I walked over to Mum and Zoe and pulled Morph out of my bag. Everyone stepped back as I activated it into a full-sized time machine.

"It's been a pleasure meeting you, Will," Luke said, saluting me as I climbed into the time machine. "I look forward to seeing you again."

The time machine door closed behind us and we began whizzing forwards in time.

"I always hated this feeling," Mum shrieked, holding on to her stomach as if she was going to puke.

Morph landed with a thump.

Suddenly, there was a tapping at the door.

"Is Eddy in there?" I heard Grandpa Monty say from outside Morph.

The time machine door flung open and Mum stepped outside.

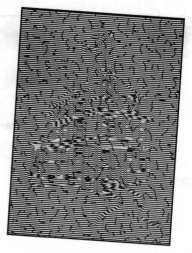

"Monty!" she smiled, giving Grandpa a big kiss on the cheek.

We'd landed in front of Solvit Hall – result!

Morph is sooo cool!

Grandpa turned red with embarrassment as Mum kissed him.

"Good to see you again, dear," Grandpa said to Mum.

Mum bent down and said hello to Plato while I deactivated Morph and watched it shrink back down to a pocket-sized time machine.

"How long have we been gone?" Zoe asked.

"About half an hour," Grandpa replied.

"What?" I gasped. "It's been months – surely."

"I'm afraid not," Grandpa said, walking back towards the house.

"I'm starving," I complained.

"Just as well I made extra beef and chocolate stew," Grandpa said, opening the door to Solvit Hall and walking through.

"Oh, Monty," Mum said. "Being in a time vortex made me miss a lot of things. And your cooking was most certainly one of them."

I noticed Mum's eyes twitch and her hands clench as she spoke – she was definitely lying about missing Grandpa's cooking.

We headed into the kitchen and sat down around the table. Grandpa served us all big bowls of stew.

"As soon as you've eaten that," Mum said, finally looking at me in disgust, "you're getting straight in the shower. When was the last time you washed?"

"I think it's better if I didn't answer that question, Mum," I said. "We were at sea for a long time and pirates aren't keen on washing."

"And we wanted to fit in," said Zoe. "The smellier you are, the better pirate you make!"

"Well you two certainly smell," Mum said, pinching her nose dramatically.

What a whiff!

That night we all stayed in Solvit Hall. Zoe slept in the spare room in the West Wing and Mum slept in the room that she always shared with Dad when we used to stay with Grandpa.

The next morning, I was the first one down to breakfast.

There was a letter waiting for me by the kettle. I opened it straight away.

HOW DO ALIENS KEEP THEIR TROUSERS ON?
WITH AN ASTEROID BELT!

ONE PARENT BACK, ONE MORE TO FIND.
VOYAGE TO THE END OF TIME, WILL.

"Is that another letter?" I heard Zoe's voice behind me.

"Morning," I said to her.

"What does it say?" she asked with a yawn.

I showed her the letter.

"Not exactly helpful," she said stating the obvious – the letters are never really that helpful.

"Good morning, kids," Mum said, walking into the kitchen with a massive smile on her face.

"Hey, Mum," I grinned. It was great having her back.

"So," she said, with her hands on her hips, "plan of action for today – how about bacon and eggs for breakfast?"

"That sounds like a great start, Mrs Solvit," Zoe replied.

"Then what?" I asked.

"Then," Mum continued, "we go and find your dad."

"Sounds like a plan, Mum," I agreed.

Mum gently pushed me and Zoe towards the

kitchen table.

"Time for breakfast first though!"

Awesome – bacon and eggs for breakfast and then Adventuring to find Dad. Sounds like a mega-good day to me!

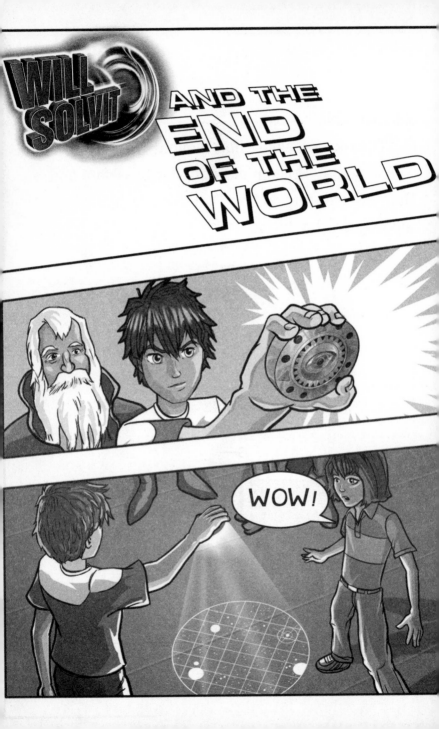

OTHER BOOKS IN THE SERIES